This book belongs to:

D1355632

**Let Me Read** is a series of books ideal for children who are starting to read. It encourages involvement of parents with children. The story can be read out aloud by the parent. The simple text encourages children to join in and the colourful illustrations help to hold their interest. Older children can read the stories by themselves.

*Level 1* - Age 5 years and above

*Level 2* - Age 6 years and above

*Level 3* - Age 7 years and above

*Level 4* - Age 8 years and above

New Dawn Press
STERLING GROUP
New Dawn Press, Inc., 244 South Randall Rd # 90, Elgin, IL 60123
e-mail: sales@newdawnpress.com

New Dawn Press, 2 Tintern Close, Slough, Berkshire, SL1-2TB, UK
e-mail: ndpuk@newdawnpress.com
sterlingdis@yahoo.co.uk

Sterling Publishers (P) Ltd.
A-59, Okhla Industrial Area, Phase-II, New Delhi-110020
e-mail: sterlingpublishers@airtelbroadband.in
ghai@nde.vsnl.net.in

Sterling Publishers Ltd. C/o Minerva Fiduciary Services (Mauritius) Limited
Suite 2004, Level 2, Alexander House, 35 Cybercity, Ebene, Mauritius
Tel: (230) 464 5100 Fax: (230) 464 3100
e-mail: uttamg@minerva.my

# Let Me Read

# Goldilocks
## and the
# Three Bears

Once there were three bears. Father Bear was a great big bear, Mother Bear was a middle-sized bear and Baby Bear was a little bear. They lived in a little house in the woods.

One morning Mother Bear made some porridge for breakfast. The porridge was too hot to eat. So the three bears went for a walk in the woods.

Goldilocks was taking a walk in the woods. She saw the little house and said, "I wonder who lives there?"

Goldilocks looked in through the window. She could see no one inside. So she opened the door and went in.

She saw a table set with
three bowls of porridge.
The porridge in the big
bowl was too hot. The
porridge in the middle-
sized bowl was too cold.

"Mmmm, this porridge tastes good!" said Goldilocks, when she ate from the little bowl.

In the next
room, she
saw three
chairs.

"This big chair is too
hard and this middle-sized
one is too soft," she said.

"This little chair is just right," said Goldilocks. But when she sat on it, the chair broke and she fell down.

In the bedroom, she saw
three beds.
"This big bed is too hard,"
she said. "And this middle-
sized bed is too soft."

"Oh, this little bed is just right!" said Goldilocks, and she fell asleep.

The bears came back
from their walk.
They saw the door open.

"Who could be there?"
they thought.

"Who has been eating my porridge?" said Father Bear.
"Who has been eating my porridge?" said Mother Bear.

Baby Bear cried out,
"Someone has eaten up all
my porridge!"

"Someone has been sitting on my chair!" growled Father Bear.

"Someone has been sitting on my chair too!" said Mother Bear.

Baby Bear sat on the floor and started crying, because his chair was broken into pieces.

In the bedroom, they saw Goldilocks fast asleep in Baby Bear's bed.

She woke up and saw the bears.

She was so scared that she got up and ran away.

# Which name goes with each picture?

- Goldilocks
- Mother Bear
- Father Bear
- Baby Bear